This book belongs to:

LEO & BLOSSOM'S
SUKKAH

LEO & BLOSSOM'S
SUKKAH

S·T·O·R·Y A·N·D P·I·C·T·U·R·E·S B·Y

JANE BRESKIN ZALBEN

HENRY HOLT AND COMPANY

New York

Copyright © 1990 by Jane Breskin Zalben
All rights reserved, including the right to reproduce this book or portions thereof in
any form. Published by Henry Holt and Company, Inc., 115 West 18th Street, New York,
New York 10011. Published in Canada by Fitzhenry and Whiteside Limited,
195 Allstate Parkway, Markham, Ontario LR 4T8.
Library of Congress Cataloging-in-Publication Data
Zalben, Jane Breskin. | Leo & Blossom's Sukkah
Summary: Brother and sister bears, Leo and Blossom,
celebrate Sukkot by building a sukkah.
[1. Sukkot—Fiction.   2. Sukkah—Fiction.   3. Bears—
Fiction.] I. Title.   II. Title: Leo and Blossom's sukkah.
PZ7.Z254Le   1990   [E]—dc20   89-24596
ISBN 0-8050-1226-5
Henry Holt books are available at special discounts
for bulk purchases for sales promotions, premiums,
fund-raising, or educational use. Special editions
or book excerpts can also be created to specification.
For details contact:
Special Sales Director | Henry Holt and Company, Inc.
115 West 18th Street   New York, New York 10011
Designed by Jane Breskin Zalben
Printed in the United States of America
1 3 5 7 9 10 8 6 4 2

To Carey Ayres—
a good friend and wonderful librarian
and
To Rahel Musleah
who makes a great sukkah!
With love

Leo and Blossom went outside to play.
They saw Papa taking sticks and tools
from the shed. Blossom asked,
"Papa, what are you doing?"
"Sukkot is coming soon," he said.
"I'm going to build the sukkah."
Leo turned to his sister, "Let's build our
own sukkah right next to Mama and Papa's."

Leo made a roof from leaves and pine boughs. Blossom wove willows between the branches. Beni came by and asked, "Can I help?" He hung many different fruits and vegetables.

Sara strung popcorn and cranberries.
Rosie made long colorful paper chains.
And their friend Max wondered aloud,
"Do you think there's too much hanging?"
But everyone was too busy to listen.

Outside the air was crisp.
Inside it smelled sweet,
like hay in a barn.
They were safe, warm, and dry.
When no one was looking, Leo
pulled an apple off a stem.

Suddenly an orange bounced on
Leo's head. Then a pear onto Beni's.
Peppers tumbled, hitting Rosie and Max.
Grapes and lemons began to roll.

Sara slipped into Blossom, who fell
as a tomato splattered on her new dress.
She began to cry. "Look at our sukkah."
Leo nudged Blossom. "We'll begin again."

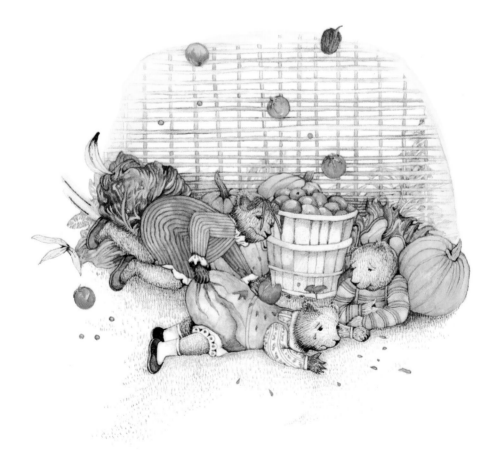

But this time their parents helped.

Later that night they had a large feast.
Everyone ate and sang. Papa told a story
about how the Jews fled Egypt and lived
in huts for forty years in the desert,
and how there was a big harvest festival
when they settled in the Land of Israel.
Blossom said, "Just like when the Pilgrims
came to America and celebrated Thanksgiving."
Papa said, "Thanksgiving is like Sukkot.
We give thanks for the first crop.
It is the holiday to ask for rain."
"Rain means life," Mama added.

Drops of water started to fall through
the twigs and leaves. Everyone looked up.
Then, outside, they heard Leo's laugh.
Mama peeked around the corner.

"Leo, get in here and shut off that hose!"
Blossom laughed. And so did all their friends,
including Mama and Papa, as they dried Leo off.

"Could we do this again next year?" Blossom asked.
Mama and Papa nodded yes. Leo smiled and said,
"Next year we'll build the sukkah even better!"
"How?" asked Blossom. "It's beautiful now."

"We'll hang pumpkins and watermelons!"
Mama and Papa just looked at Leo and sighed.
"Okay, Indian corn and squash," Leo said.
"To next year!" Everyone chimed in.

The moonlight cast shadows in the stillness.
Stars twinkled between the boughs above.
As the family fell asleep, they heard the
gentle pitter-patter of rain.

SUKKOT

Sukkot is the Festival of Booths, or Tabernacles. It is a joyous festival that commemorates the final gathering of the harvest. At Sukkot a temporary hut (or booth) is built. In it a family eats, drinks, and sleeps during the holiday, and is reminded of how the Israelites lived in the wilderness. The hut may have three sides or four, with walls of bamboo poles or canvas, and a loose roof of tree branches of evergreens or palms. The covering of branches should be heavy enough for there to be shade during the day, but open enough for the stars to be seen at night.

In her right hand Blossom carries a *lulav* (or palm branch) attached to two willow boughs and three myrtle branches; in her left hand she carries an *etrog* (or citrus fruit). These are the four festival symbols, called the Four Species: palm, willow, myrtle, and citron. The waving of the *lulav* in different directions symbolizes that God is everywhere.

In 1620, when the Pilgrims came to America, they held a harvest festival. They based their first Thanksgiving on the ancient holiday of Sukkot.

etrog (or citrus fruit)

lulav (or palm branch)

THE SUKKAH

FRUITS AND VEGETABLES YOU CAN HANG IN THE SUKKAH

The Seven Major Fruits of Israel are:

wheat

olives

barley

dates

grapes

figs

pomegranates

Leo and Blossom and their friends also hung or brought in:

paper chains

oranges

popcorn

apples

cranberries

lemons

peppers

peaches

gourds

pears

tomatoes

corn

pumpkins

beets

cabbages

carrots